Writerly Curiosities

A Canadian anthology of poetry and prose prompted by
treasures in the mail

edited by Janet Whitehead

Musings and Mud Enterprises

Musings and Mud Enterprises
830 Pleasant Street
Kamloops BC V2C 3B5

Contents

Treasures in the mail

S TRANGE COINS, CRUMPLED PAPER, antique watches
– a few of many little treasures shipped to a curious
collective of writers, challenging them to tell us a story.

They are the writers of the Damn Book Done group.
They had Writerly Kits in common—a subscription box
that arrived full of items to inspire their writing. They also
had in common, a desire to spend time with their words,
sneaking past inner critics, perfectionism, and all that can
stop them, to get their damn books done.

It seemed only right that they got one damn book done
together, don't you think?

And here it is, a collection of poetry and prose prompted
by those treasures that landed in the writers' mailboxes.

A Poem, maybe

Coreena McBurnie

WHAT IF I HAD a mission with my writing? And could express myself clearly, elegantly, and with flashes of brilliance?

What if exhilarating ideas lapped persistently like the waves on the shore?

What if the patina of my doubt shone with a purple-golden aura, drawing the eye, transforming uncertainty to insight? A spice market of colours and smells to explore and combine in delicious combinations?

What if I wrote something cozy and soothing, something that would chamomile-tea-envelop comfort another in their misty, drizzly fog?

What if I light that hearth-fire ember to warm and brighten on a chilly, dark day, illuminating some truth for myself that may be a mirror for another?

What if I was my own sun, a supernova eruption of insight and deep thoughts and frivolity and entertainment?

What if I walked away from my Sisyphean boulder, letting it thunder down the hill, crushing my doubts, fears, and blocks? What if I took that step sideways instead of trudging up?

What if I let go of the oars and sit and write?

ele

Prompt: Paint Chip Poetry prompts

Misty Morning Meanderings

Kristy Janota

C ONSCIOUSNESS SEEPS IN WITH the mellow light. My eyelids mask the majority of light but not all. I roll over in escape. My thoughts swirl with unclear origins. I feel like there is something to be done but it's just out of grasp. Emotions mingling on the surface, ebb away.

My boat is riding high on the crest of a wave as the sun peeks over the muted horizon. The sails are full and the breeze feels like cool silk across my skin. I see calmer seas ahead. I sigh deep and allow my shoulders to fall away from my ears. The small corrections through the night have us on a better trajectory. The team was efficient, though battled against the weather, through the night. We had poured over our options, trusted the wariness we felt, and seemed to have made some good choices. No land in sight yet but, if our calculated adjustments prove correct, we will arrive in safe harbour by night fall. Movement catches my eye off the port side. I grab the binoculars slung over my arm. Was it a manta ray or a dolphin? I scan slowly and spot one crest the water again. It is a ray. Its sleek, broad silhouette gracefully dips back below the surface. I don't think there is much more satisfying than to glimpse our neighbours as we cross this cobalt sea. I see more ripples and keep focused ahead.

The peacefulness is disrupted by a piercing sound. What was I doing? I shift around and fumble to get it to stop. That sound, sharp and repetitive, really is jarring. I should change that. There is something I'm supposed to be doing but I settle again. I'm just going to enjoy the quiet a bit longer and I drift.

The beach glitters in the soft sunlight. The sand feels cool between my toes as I walk near the water's edge. The air feels like early morning bringing the peacefulness of a new day. The waves seem to breathe along with me, lapping softly at my feet which temporarily imprint the pliable sand. The salt air soothes. I wonder vaguely where this place might be. Not a soul in sight. The trees and undergrowth protect the entire bay, creating solitude, though the muted sounds coming from the forest hint at abundant life. My eyes catch some movement in the sand up ahead. Tiny flailing limbs flap as a little turtle fumbles toward safety. He's working with determination and he takes no notice of me approaching. I lift him gently by his sides while his limbs keep flailing and deliver him to the water. He disappears into the froth, so much faster now in the water. My gaze aims to follow, but he's gone. This place has such a calmness to it, I should really come here more often. Sometimes I swim here but today I just want to feel grounded and peaceful with my feet in the sand.

I am so preoccupied by my little friend that I don't notice someone standing nearby. I see him and smile. His presence is calming and nurturing and I'm not feeling as concerned as one might think to see someone who had been gone for so long. Grandpa grins at me and I link my arm through his as we fall into step. It is a while before I speak but the quiet feels nourishing. "What brings you here today?" I ask.

"I'm always here in my own way. Or you could say, a thought away," he replies. "This place is an ideal meeting ground. It's like the peacefulness and positivity create a space beyond earthy boundaries." He asks, "How did it feel to let the turtle go?"

"It felt right. Like my part was to give a helping hand but then let go," I answer.

"This parallels life," he says. "People will come into your life and need a little boost but after, they aren't your responsibility. They need to swim on their own. You are meant to help but not be responsible for them." And with that remark he fades away, as do the water and sand.

I squint into the morning light and wonder what time it is. I'm blasted again and silence the incessant reminders. I feel like my limbs are made of dense clay. I'm so warm and nestled, I never want to move. I shift and turn away from the soft filtered sunlight, ignoring my nagging responsibilities as I sink into the warmth.

The vibrant white light is shining directly on me, blinding me momentarily. The energy of it is palpable as it flows through me and straight into the earth. I feel the charged celestial quality of the white light followed by the warmth of the earth's response, like a slow rising glow. The energy is reciprocated through me creating a circuit type connection. The burst of colliding energy has an electric quality. I feel myself rising, away from the ground though deeply rooted at the same time. I see a tree forming around me; large, old growth, but new in its bloom. The leaves open and broaden, collecting the light. The connection I feel is here, that circuit. The energy from above and below allows the tree to progress to full bloom before my eyes. The colors are gentle like soft, glowing pastels though breathtaking with an iridescent quality. I can walk the thick wide branches and follow them to the center. I see people are using the healing nature of the tree to create leaf hammocks for their patients. I recognize many here who, in slumber, are finding some rejuvenation and well-being. I'll have to ask them how they are feeling ...when I see them next. I find my own healing hammock and settle in.

Blast, blast, blast. I feel the glow fading and stretch vaguely. That sound! So irritating. Off it goes. I'm amused that I may be a little too efficient at shutting it down. I can't help it, I'm just too comfortable and my mind wanders again.

After hours of searching, I can hear rhythmic ticking. Our tactical bomb unit was put out on assignment after the frantic calls came in. We got everyone out of the building.

Now, hopefully we can save the structure too. It's getting louder, we must be getting close.

"Over here," I yell, "it must be in that cabinet."

Our Commander's voice is firm through my earbuds, "Careful! Slowly open it, do you see it?"

"Yes, it's here" I responded.

"How many minutes are left?" she said.

"10...and it's complex," my voice is thick.

"Ok, I'll talk you through it," she responded.

"I've removed the casing. There are many canisters. This one could clear the entire block. Yes, the wires are accessible, they are all grey this time."

"Look at the configuration," my commander prompts.

"Yes, I see the pattern, and have located the correct wire."

"Are you all in agreement?" the commander confirms.

"Yes, it's the bottom one and I'm ready to cut when you are. Has everyone cleared the area?"

"Yes, all clear," she answered.

"1,2,3... oh THANK MARY MOTHER OF GOD! We got it!" I exclaim as adrenaline courses through me. I close my eyes and allow my heartbeat to slow. The scene slips away and I'm transported again.

I find myself walking in the forest along a soft dirt path. I hear the familiar rush. The cascading water is a refreshing sound. I make my way to the base of the falls where a smooth flat boulder creates the perfect platform under the veil of water. The water is an ideal temperature as it washes over me, warm and soothing. It has a purifying quality and leaves me feeling clear mentally and physically. I catch movement as I open my eyes, as she leans casually against a tree.

"Oh, hello, my good friend! I wondered if you would come," I remark as I step out of the water. "What words of wisdom do you have for me?"

"You know you could use more sleep..." she said with humour in her voice.

"I know, might make mornings a little easier," I grin back.

"Great work with the clean eating," she said, "now add clean thinking."

"Would you care to elaborate?" I counter.

She replied "Don't muddy your thoughts with doubts, worries, sadness. Find the love, acceptance and appreciation for yourself and everyone else - you all deserve it - there is peace in that."

"True," I let those words sink in, "Thanks for the inspiration and wisdom, I'm lucky to have you."

Blast Blast. I'm pulled awake again. I'm so tired! What was I dreaming about? It's like a fog is rolling though my brain. The dreams are there but just out of focus. How long have I been pressing snooze? I open my bleary eyes and will them to focus. Wow! I seriously overslept... wasn't there a waterfall? I could go for that now, surely that would jolt me awake! No more snooze...

Prompt: magical adventure

The Uncrumpling of a Creative Kid

JANET L WHITEHEAD

MS. BELL DID NOT have a recycle monitor in her classroom. Sometimes the children complained because other classrooms had recycling monitors. The monitors got to leave the classroom into near empty hallways at the end of each day to dump the recycling container. Those kids got to have a little chat with friends at the bins and take their time wandering back to class. Sometimes they would do fancy steps along the way to hear the music the echo of their footsteps made. It seemed like fun to Ms. Bell's students.

"I do more clean-up after you leave," Ms. Bell told the children, "It makes sense that I take the recycle out after that." They'd groan but accept her decision.

Monday's end of the day ritual began as always. Ms. Bell made a fresh coffee in the staff room and brought it back to her desk. She placed the nearly full recycling bin beside her, had a sip of her coffee, and started digging. Ms. Bell learned a lot about her students as she examined the items in the container. She would learn what a child was struggling with by a crumpled-up math sheet. She'd learn what they disliked when "I HATE THIS" was penned across an abandoned story assignment. She'd get an idea of the latest trends in snacks by the wrappers tossed out, and the latest trends in disliked snacks when the wrappers still had food in them. She'd even learn about the joys and upsets of home life. Last week, a note with a wish to make Granny well was a valuable find and Ms. Bell was able to provide more support. Ms. Bell loved her apres-school coffee and recycling breaks.

A large piece of sketch paper, crumpled as small as it could be, took up half the space at the bottom of the bin. Ms. Bell was very curious as she unfolded it. The paper was by far a better quality than she could provide in the classroom. As each crease and crinkle were released, Ms. Bell held her breath in wonder. When it was finally opened onto her desk, she gasped.

There was a commotion the next morning as the children arrived in class. Backpacks were dropped randomly on the floor as children sprinted to see the new artwork on the special art wall – the wall that hosted artworks lent to the classroom by artists or by the local gallery.

"Wow!" children said. "Ohh, that's amazing!" Some children just stared in awe. Others declared their love of the piece quite emphatically. There were others who weren't interested at all, but that's how it goes with art.

Ms. Bell had gently centered the crumpled drawing on a large black canvas that had been tucked in the storage room.

"Who made this?" children asked.

Ms. Bell simply said, "A local artist, I believe. It is wonderful, isn't it? What makes it so compelling, do you think?"

"The moon! It's like the light from the moon is dancing down a pathway in the forest!"

"The unusual shape of the trees!"

"It's like a sculpture on a canvas – the way the corners lift up!"

"I like all the wrinkles. The artist did it to add texture, right?"

Ms. Bell said she wasn't sure but added, "The principal has asked for this to be hung in the main lobby but I thought for one day, we'd keep it here."

Brady kept glancing at his artwork so prominently placed on the wall. The crinkles made it look like the light from the moon rays were leaping off the canvas and the dark was hiding in the creases. He liked it. Ms. Bell was being silly, though. It wasn't that good. Some of the kids didn't like it, he could tell. And it wasn't good enough to show his parents. They would smile and say something like 'That's okay. But it is important for you to become a master at a skill. Work harder." Brady knew this is what they would say. They say it to his brother, Evan, when he plays his violin.

Sometimes he is pretty sure they scowl when his sister doesn't score in her soccer game. Brady thinks it's easier to have no skills than to have his parents' disapproval, plus he doesn't even want to imagine the teasing his siblings would hand him if they saw his art.

Brady's parents do not know that under his mattress there are sketchbooks, pens, pencils, watercolours and brushes all laid out neatly. They do not know that his grandmother purchases these items that he sneaks into the house. Bedtime is the best time of day: Brady pulls out his art supplies and disappears into colour and lines and other worlds until his eyes will no longer stay open.

Brady did not claim ownership of the artwork at school but that night he pulled out his very best paper, the Arches 150 lb watercolour pad. Just maybe his work is worthy of this good paper, he thought. He will do his best and maybe tomorrow he'll give it to his teacher.

One pencil line followed another and another but they did not connect right. What if the kids hate it? Brady tried adding colour but the paints flowed into a muddy mess. He slammed down his brush in frustration and for the first time in a long time he went to bed before his eyes were too sleepy to stay open.

The next morning, he crumpled the disastrous drawing into a ball of sorts. The heavy paper was harder to crumple than his usual paper. Still, he crammed it in his backpack and this time tossed it in the big recycle bin near the corner store. That's where most of his projects went. He never wanted his parents or his siblings to find his work. He'd just been in a rush yesterday, which is why his artwork ended up in a bin at school. He was never going to do that again.

Ms. Bell caught up to Brady in the school hallway. "Did you see we moved the new artwork into the lobby?" she asked.

Brady said nothing.

"Do you like it?" Ms. Bell asked.

"Um. It's okay, I guess," he answered before dropping his head and scooting away.

That night, Brady decided to try again. He liked that his teacher and some of his classmates liked his artwork. He liked how it looked, mounted on the black canvas. Even the crinkles were cool. The Arches paper came out once more and resulted in 45 minutes of frustration. Brady set his tools down and sat quietly for a few minutes. Suddenly, he reached under his mattress to grab his usual paper, the lighter weight paper he was used to. He sketched out images and drizzled colour into well thought out spaces. He forgot that he was trying to create art to actually show someone and he, once again, fell into that magical flow that was his creative process. His paper filled with silhouette dancers circling a golden sun, ending only when his eyes drooped shut.

In the morning, Brady eagerly checked his artwork. He was disappointed. It wasn't good enough, he thought, and he crumpled it up and tucked it in his backpack. Once more, his artwork was tossed into the huge recycle bin on his way to school.

When Brady arrived at class the following day, though, there was his artwork, once again mounted on a black canvas, the golden sun shimmering, the silhouettes deepened in the creases of the crinkled paper. He could not believe how good it looked, nor that it was in his classroom on the special wall again.

Once again, his classmates raved about the artwork, while Ms. Bell chatted on about the mysterious artist and their fascinating painting techniques. Evan and Jenna made fun of it, saying it was silly to use wrinkled paper.

Again, Brady did not lay claim to the artwork. Instead he anxiously watched the clock waiting for the 3 o'clock bell. First out the door, he raced home and announced he was tired and was going to go lay down for a while. He snuck his art supplies out from under his mattress and set up a corner to paint in his closet. If someone came in to check on him, he could quickly close the closet door.

With no plan in mind, he dropped paint onto his paper. The blob was a good start to a piano shape, he noted, and with ink, pencil and paint, he created a scene with a decrepit old piano being hugged by a forest of tall cedar-like trees. He liked it. He thought of Evan and Jenna and if they would like it without the crinkles. His stomach felt sour thinking of them not liking his work. He sat staring at his art for a while. Finally, he decided he did like the crinkle texture in the artwork at school so he crumpled it up, this time lovingly, and tucked it in his backpack for morning.

Try as he may, he could not bring himself to deliver his artwork to his teacher. Habit and fear had him toss it into the big recycling bin at the store once again. He hoped it would be okay, that somehow it got salvaged again.

By the next morning, he regretted that decision. His artwork did not show up magically mounted on a canvas in his classroom. He wondered how often that big bin got emptied and if he might be able to save his work after school. The day dragged long, until early afternoon when Ms. Bell made an announcement.

"Class, exciting news! Today a reporter from Town News is coming to do a news clip about the mysterious artworks. She would like our class to meet her in the lobby to interview us about our thoughts about the works."

Brady knew climbing out the window and running away would be more noticeable than quietly melting into a line-up of kids eager to be on the news. He shrunk into the group as best he could, making himself as invisible as possible. This was scary.

The orderly line-up broke into chaos as they neared the lobby.

"Another one!" the children yelled, racing to see the third artwork. "Look! Look at it!" they called out.

The reporter was snapping photos of the children's enthusiastic response. A camera person was following their movements. And Brady, he lagged behind, stunned to see his third artwork centered between his other two, spotlights on either side. The piano in the painting looked almost angelic, like the creases highlighted a halo around it. The tree branches looked deep and serious wrapped warmly around the piano.

He scanned the group for Evan and Jenna. They didn't look very interested. Brady looked at his work again. Maybe his work did suck after all.

"Coming?" Ms. Bell said to Brady, scooting him along to the lobby.

The reporter set her camera down and picked up a mic. "This artwork is quite a mystery. Tell me, what do you think of the art?" She asked several children their opinions on the style of art, who they thought the artist was, and why the art kept mysteriously showing up. She chatted with the principal and, of course, Ms. Bell. But Brady wasn't paying attention to all of that. He was worried the reporter would talk to the kids who didn't like his work. Then, even worse, he spotted his parents, off to the side of the crowd, looking quite bewildered.

The reporter walked over to his parents. "As parents, - you are parents, correct? - what is your opinion of this mysterious art?"

Brady's Dad stumbled a bit, "Oh, well, I'm just here for a parent/teacher meeting. The art...well, it's quite good..."

"Amazing," Brady's Mom interrupted, "The colour combinations are stunning. And the way the texture catches the light - such a unique style. Who is the artist?"

Ms. Belle stepped forward. "A local artist," she said, "I'm hoping the artist will share who they are sometime." She doesn't even glance at Brady, but he knows she knows.

Brady summoned every bit of courage he had and raised one finger on his hand. Not enough for anyone to see, though. He shuffled uncomfortably then whispered, "Me."

"Pardon, son?" Brady's Dad said.

"Me!" Brady blurted out in his outdoor voice.

The entire lobby quieted as all eyes turn to Brady.

"I've been afraid to tell you," Brady looked pleadingly at his parents, "It's not very good."

"What do you mean, Brady?" his mom looked confused, "I don't understand."

Dad stepped towards Brady. He knelt down. "Brady, I don't understand either. I didn't think you still liked doing art. You drew so much when you were small."

"I thought you lost interest," Mom added.

"I thought... well, I dunno, you never said much about it," Brady responded.

Mom was quiet for a moment. The whole room silently watched as she as thoughtfully replied, "I loved art when I was kid, Brady. I stopped because my mother always criticized me. Your dad and I never wanted to be like that with you."

"We didn't want to influence how you felt about your art. That's what is important." Dad said, and with a little grimace he added, "That kinda backfired, I guess."

"But Grama buys me art supplies!" Brady answered.

"What? That makes no sense!" Mom blurted out, then looked around embarrassed because so many people were listening.

"Grama always says the least she can do now is help one artist in the family," Brady explained.

Brady's parents looked at one another, bewilderment, then understanding, expressed in unspoken words.

"Brady, I'm so proud of you. You know, it's not easy being an artist. It's easier to quit than to worry about what people think. But you didn't quit. Do you think you could help me get back to doing art?" Mom asked with a warm smile.

Brady's eyes lit up, "Yeah, yeah, that'd be cool." He added confidently, "Yes, I can help you."

"A great reveal here at Riverside School," the reporter chimed in in her announcer's voice, "Our mysterious artist is this young fellow. Brady, correct? Tell us, Brady, how do you create your art? How do you get your ideas? How do you add the creases in your art? It's a very unique style that the whole town will soon be talking about."

Brady shuffled his feet a bit, but with a smile he just couldn't stop and a twinkle in his eyes, he replied, "I don't know. It just happens. When I make it, I don't think the art is good. I crumple it up. Then it appears at school and I think it's not too bad."

Ms. Bell beamed at her young student. "It's damn good," she announced, far too loudly because now the whole classroom and the principal have heard her swear. The reaction, though, is simply giggles and laughter and both children and adults commenting in agreement.

Ms. Bell pulled Brady aside while the reporter turned to interview the parents. Brady heard his mom say how hard it can be to be creative, how sensitive artists can be. But then Ms. Bell gave him a hug. "Will I need to be picking up the recycle at the store still? Or might you bring your artwork all the way to school now?"

"I'll bring it to school," he said, "Crumpled. But maybe sometimes not crumpled. Wait, maybe I'll try crumpling the paper first then paint it…" At that, Brady's imagination went wild with the possibilities for his art projects. "I'll try with my best paper, too. Maybe a whale scene next. Dad, Mom, can we go now? We have some painting to do!"

ele

Prompt: Crumpled paper

Daugre

JESSICA HEWLETT

LIGHT EXPLODED BEFORE MY eyes with a tumultuous clatter of metal as I spun through the air. This didn't feel right.

The wind ripped past, but not against my skin and when I blinked there was no flicker of eyelids. The ground approached fast and I stretched out my hands, but nothing happened. Instead, I hit the ground, bounced back into the air and flipped several times before landing back with a metallic clink.

I stared uncomprehendingly at the destroyed room before me. What had just happened? I reached for memory, but all I found was darkness. I didn't even remember my name.

I took a breath and that's when it hit me. There was no movement of air, no expansion of lungs. The body I expected was from ages past. These hard edges I felt now, the coldness that sat in my core, that was my truth. My body was a coin.

I scrambled at the past that refused to come forth, at the panic that clawed at my nonexistent throat. Was this a mistake? A curse? A punishment? A vocation?

I searched the room for clues, but all I got were more questions.

Obviously, I was in a living room, but its contents had been tossed. Chairs were turned over and books spilled across the floor littered with splinters of glass and porcelain. Sprawled across the floor, partially hidden by a coffee table was an old man. Blood trickled down his forehead into thin grey hair. I knew this man, recognized the curve of his nose and the grey that glinted in his pain shrouded eyes.

There was a shift of weight behind me, then a clattering as someone knelt into view. She would have been pretty if it hadn't been for the bags pulling at her blood-shot eyes. Cursing under her breath, she scooped up errant coins with shaking hands and dropped them into a rusty coffee can.

I cringed, knowing that blackened space too well. I didn't want to go back. I looked to Jacob, but his eyes were closed, there'd be no help from him.

There was no more time, the woman's hand swept towards me in a tidal wave of coins. Helpless to its force, gravity shifted, spun, and then I was falling with glints of silver and gold. I clinked into darkness and quickly became buried under tumbling coins.

I screamed, but there was only silence. As darkness became complete, terror took hold.

Light pierced through my nightmare. I was falling again. I struggled against the lingering visions of frothing blood to find a sunlit room that tumbled around me. Voices crescendoed over top as I collided with the ground. I rolled to a stop, propped up against a table leg.

I fought against the confusion as I took in my new surroundings. The coffee tin lay on the ground, coins and jewellery spilled out between the woman and a boy in his early teens.

"You lied," whispered the boy.

"These are mine," she said, waving to the scattered coins.

"Grandpa wasn't in the war," he said, scooping a medal off the pile, "Grandpa was blind as a bat."

The woman snatched it out of the boy's hand. "Henric, mind your own business and go to school. You're going to be late."

"Dad said if he catches you again...," continued Henric, his voice catching.

They both looked up at the ceiling and I realized I could hear water running. Suddenly, the sound stopped.

"Go. To. School," snapped his mother.

Henric folded his arms over his chest. "And what if I stay, Shanice," he sneered the last word. "What are you going to do about it?"

She strangled a scream. "I'm your Mother, god damn it. You will listen to me."

"You've been failing that job for years."

Her slap froze inches from his face and as the seconds ticked by, I realized that it was me holding her. As soon as I mentally let go, she stumbled back a step.

Henric touched his unmarked cheek, like it stung.

"If you do that," she continued, voice shaking, eyes flicking upstairs, "then you will be the one to destroy this family."

Henric jerked back then bolted from the room, an outer door slamming seconds later.

The mother dropped to her knees, sobs shaking her as she frantically scooped the coins and jewellery back into the tin. I lay far enough away that her hand moved past me with her unaware of leaving me behind. The blankness of my past told me nothing, but instinct thrummed inside me. I couldn't be left behind.

I flexed the metal of my being, altering it, while also manipulating the morning light. Shanice blinked away the errant sun and her eyes landed on me. She scooped me up and I lay against her warm palm, her finger sliding along my surface.

"You're...different," she said. I waited as the rosy darkness of her hand closed around me. Would I be relegated to the hell of the tin or would she keep me closer.

Minutes later, I settled against her shirt, hung from the hole I'd earlier created. Beside me was a #1 Mom pendant that held both hope and sorrow.

Shanice shoved the tin into a backpack, then rushed to look out the front window. Outside was a street lined with houses and fancy automobiles I'd never seen the like before. Down the street was a white emergency vehicle, stripped blue and red with lights flashing on its roof. She cursed. I didn't understand the problem, but she turned away before I got a chance to observe more. She left the house through the back, careful to close the door quietly.

I tried tracking Shanice's movements along the suburban streets, but the puzzle of her being was distracting. Her emotions were a maze of dead ends and as I searched, I realized something was wrong. I could sense a faint rot.

Was this the source of the divide between Henric and his mother?

Further investigation became impossible when Shanice stepped into a rancid, cluttered house.

The living room was a mess of greasy boxes and dirty dishes. Sitting in an upholstered chair was an overweight man, old sweat stained against the armpits of his shirt. It wasn't the state of the room that had disturbed me, but this man.

"What do you got for me?" he said, scratching at his greasy hair. His eyes never left the animated box across from him.

"It's good stuff," Shanice's words rushed out. Her hands shook as she fumbled with the clasp on the backpack.

"You know you still owe me." I wanted to get out of here. This man didn't have rot like Shanice, but there was something else.

"There's enough here for that and for one more hit."

I recognized his type. He was a predator, but not in the traditional sense of a wolf. He was like a weasel. I was the wolf. I paused, startled by my statement. I was a wolf? No, I was a coin, wasn't I?

Shanice finally conquered the backpack and pulled out the tin.

"Don't be wasting my time with costume jewellery," snarled the man.

"No, no, this is better," her finger reached up and smoothed over my warm surface. She shouldn't be here, I suddenly decided. This man was the feeder of the rot growing inside her.

She placed the tin on the table between them and opened the lid revealing the dull matte of tarnished coins. The man snorted and combed his fingers through the coins, picking up a few, then dropping them in disgust.

"These are nothing but centennials. You'd be lucky if there was a couple dollars worth here."

"It's good stuff," she pleaded. "He had it all on display, see these," she pulled bills sandwiched in plastic sleeves from her back pocket. The buyer sat up straighter and I felt the rot inside Shanice quicken and pulse.

I had to stop this. I couldn't muffle the rot, but I felt I had other influences.

The man reached for the bills just as I pushed towards him. He hesitated, hand hovering, "Where did you steal these from," his voice was wary and he looked over her shoulder.

She followed his gaze to the window of an empty street. "It was just a nobody, no one to worry about." She pushed the bills towards his hand.

"If this was a collector, then he would have catalogued it, recorded the serial numbers," he pulled his hand away. "You take it to the broker, bring me real cash instead."

Shanice shrank back, "You get a better rate than me," her voice was smaller. "I won't have enough if I sell it to him."

"Not my problem." His attention was back to the moving picture, but his eyes kept twitching to the window. I don't know what I did, but it was working.

"Take the coins and this watch," she said, pulling the old watch from her pocket. "I just need another hit. I won't make it through the day."

"No, your stuff is dirty," snapped the man. "You got a bank account. You got a hardworking man, take it from him."

"But..."

"Get out," the man said, louder.

Shanice flinched like she'd been hit and I boosted the fear quivering inside her. She clasped the jewellery box to her chest and bolted out of the house.

I twirled slowly in the air, sunlight glinting off of my surface. Shanice's face, then Henric's spun into view in a spiralling pendulum.

"This is for you, Henric," their faces spun by, silence spread between them.

"You're right," she said. "I let things slip, but I promise I'm trying harder this time." Henric's hard face met Shanice's pleading eyes.

"Come downstairs for dinner," she said even quieter. "I made your favourite." The pendulum ceased as I was laid on a desk, beside his closed fist. A moment later, a door clicked shut.

Henric's face appeared over mine, blocking out walls covered with posters. His finger slid over the raised metal that covered my surface. I wondered what it was. By instinct, I thought animal, but I couldn't pinpoint which one. Horse, wolf, eagle, even a griffin or dragon felt possible.

I'd decided to switch people once Shanice had returned home. She was not for me. Her core rot was a hinderance, so I did what I could for her, then convinced her to give me to Henric.

I floated through the air as Henric picked me up and after a moment's hesitation, clasped the chain around his neck. He snagged the crumpled business card he'd been hiding, then tucked me under his shirt, muffling my sight.

Dinner was a blind affair that grated at me.

"It's been ages since you made this," said Henric's dad, his cutlery clanking against his plate.

"I know, hon. I was thinking about that today and decided it was time to get out of my rut," her voice was happy, cheerful, but I could sense something underneath. It was connected to the rot, but wasn't of the rot. It didn't make sense.

"Do you need more gravy, Henric?" she continued. "You've barely touched your salisbury steak.

Henric shifted and his knife screeched across the plate as he cut in.

"Whaddya say, buddy," said Dad.

"It's good, thanks," Henric said, mouth full.

Dinner continued with stilted chatter, and cleanup was equally awkward as Dad tried asking about Henric's day. He gave up after the continued single word replies.

When Henric finally left the kitchen, I expected him to head upstairs, but his momentum didn't ascend.

Behind him in the kitchen, I could hear his parents talking, his father getting ready to leave for his night shift.

I was getting frustrated with the lack of vision. You'd think my endless darkness would have made me immune to blindness, but it was having the opposite effect.

Henric's body changed, I felt his need for smallness and quiet. His footsteps became slow and soft and I fretted over my inability to see. I knew there had to be a way around this. I could feel it in my hidden memories, but it was just out of my reach.

Henric stepped into a room, his parent's conversation now muffled. He moved furtively through the room and I could hear him shifting things around. Cursing this thin piece of cotton. I urged him to pull me free, but all he did was absently rub at me through the cloth, before continuing with his search.

The frustration welled inside me and as I rode the wave of it, my vision finally eased through the fabric. Had it really been that easy?

I recognized this room from this morning. This was where Mom had threaded me on her chain. Henric was searching through her items, pushing books aside on the shelves, looking behind the futon and lifting cushions.

I knew what he was looking for and understood the sadness that had been welling in his heart all through dinner. I searched with him and gave him a nudge towards the bay window when I saw the tell-tale rust of the tin. He pushed the plants aside, revealing the coffee tin nestled amongst the aralia and ivy. Henric replaced the plants then stepped out the side door, his parents still in the kitchen.

Five minutes later, he was knocking at the house where this all began.

The old man opened the door, a bandage taped along his forehead.

"Whaddya want," Jacob asked, his voice thick with age, then his eyes dropped to the tin.

"I'm sorry," started Henric, "my..."

"Shut up and give it to me," he said, hands outstretched.

Henric handed it over and followed the old man into the living room. The mess had been cleaned up, but his display cases were empty and the mantle's patchy dust revealed the imprint of missing items.

The old man placed the tin on the dining room table. "You got a right ole' cunt of a mother, know that, boy?" he said as he opened the lid to a mess of coins.

I could feel the shock and anger ripple through Henric, but I wasn't surprised. This was the Jacob I knew.

"She's been having a hard time lately," Henric tried.

"Haven't we all," interrupted Jacob, "but what she's having a hard time with is harming everyone else," he said as he grabbed a handful of coins and spilled them across the table. He checked every coin, before returning for more.

After his final handful, he slapped his hand against the table, the coins bouncing from the force. "This isn't all of them. She sold some, didn't she?"

Henric's hand reached for his shirt and told the story without saying a word.

Jacob stalked over. "Get that thing off your neck and hand it over."

"She gave it to me," Henric's voice quavered.

"Sure, and you knew it was stolen. What does that make you?"

Henric's fingers closed around my surface. "You can't take it. I won't let you."

Jacob grunted and stared at us, before dropping into a chair. "That thing's a curse, boy, nothing good ever comes of it.

"No," I yelled.

Henric clutched at his head, while Jacob only scowled.

"Waking up, Daugre? You ain't done me any good. Got my leg near blown off 'cause of you. Wish you'd let me drop you into that blasted ocean."

"What are you talking about?" asked Henric, his voice weak.

"I kept you alive," I said, "You had a larger purpose."

"I never asked for that purpose," Jacob yelled, voice going hoarse. "You're just a parasite, leeching off of us, since who knows how long."

"It's just a coin," Henric whispered.

"Then both of us are crazy, cause we're hearing the same voice in our head now, aren't we." Jacob raked his fingers through his thin hair, making it stick up wildly. "This coin is old, by many generations, all the way back to the Celts."

With his words, I felt the darkness lighten in mind and the haze of memories sat at the edge of my consciousness. What he said was right and questions burned to be released, but I held them tight. This wasn't the time.

"I just wanted to make right what she did," Henric said, ignorant of my growing epiphany.

Jacob's eyes softened. "But it's not good enough, is it?" he sighed.

"What do you mean? I returned the coins?"

"And Daugre's still tied around your neck, means you ain't done growing yet."

Henric's hand dropped to his pocket. "I don't understand."

"Yes, you do and Daugre's currently too dimwitted to do more than nudge you."

Anger flushed within me.

Jacob suddenly laughed, "Guess we're still connected, I felt that."

"I did to," whispered Henric.

"Oh hell," complained Jacob. "I thought I was done with this bullshit." He looked up at the ceiling, exhaling a breath.

"Fine," Jacob continued. "There's something you need to do and it's up to you to figure it out. The sooner you do it, the sooner you'll be free of Daugre. I think." The last words were barely audible.

Henric stood there for a moment, staring at the carpet pile. Finally, he looked at Jacob. "Could I use your phone?"

Five minutes later, we stood outside Henric's house. He'd phoned the number on the card he'd been hiding and left a message explaining what his mother had done. When he'd stepped out of Jacob's house, we were surprised to see flashing lights down the street.

Henric raced over but slid to a stop when he saw his mom being hauled out of the house in hand-cuffs.

Her face was streaked with mascara. "I swear, I had it," she said as they helped her down the stairs. "I hid it, but now it's gone."

Henric stood on the sidewalk, a few feet from a police car. An officer was standing by it, a phone to his ear. He turned and made eye contact.

"Henric?" he asked, lowering his phone.

"I just left the message," Henric said, hoarsely. "How did you get here so fast."

"Your mom called us."

"Henric!" wailed his mom. "I just couldn't do it anymore. I knew I was just going to keep doing it, but now...I won't be able to now." She ducked her head as the officer guided her into the back of the police car.

"But..." Henric's voice trailed of.

The officer looked over Henric's shoulder. "Mr. Janovich, did you still want to press charges."

Henric turned around to see the old man hobbling towards them. "No," he said, "just a waste of time. All that matters is I've got my stuff back."

The officer stepped away and Henric turned back to his mom crying in the back of the car. Jacob placed his hand on the boy's shoulder. It was light, but his fingers dug in with a hint of his former strength.

"Come on back to my house," Jacob said. "You can wait for your dad there."

Prompt: coin

Last Train to Seinäjoki

SHAWN L. BIRD

"T HE PRICE OF A ticket is forty markka," Kirsi told me. "The train leaves from Tampere at 16.43."

"I'll be on it," I assured her as I hung up the phone.

I was visiting my penpal in Western Finland, at last. We had been matched through the International Post Box of the World Association of Girl Guides and Girl Scouts years before. Me, a twelve year old Girl Guide in Kelowna, Canada. Kirsi, a twelve year old Partiolainen in Seinäjoki, Finland. We had written faithfully through our teens, and much to my surprise, Rotary had chosen Finland for me to live on a Youth Exchange year. I had been in the country for a few months when we began planning a trip for me to stay with her family for a week in April.

I lived on the Southeast coast, on an island in the Gulf of Finland. Kirsi's home was in the West, on the Gulf of Bothnia, five hundred kilometres was certainly closer than seven thousand, but even though I was in the country, it was still letters for us until we braved one phone call before my departure. My Finnish was okay and her English was good. Details prepared. Off I went, but I forgot to go to the bank before I left. In my wallet I had just enough for the train ticket, but I wasn't going to be able to buy anything else until I could visit a bank in Seinäjoki. Just fifty markka in my wallet. About twelve dollars Canadian.

One of my sponsor Rotarians had a bus company, so I was given two bus passes for the year. One was for local buses. One allowed travel to some of the major cities. I was using my free pass to get from Kotka to Tampere, and then I was going to take the electric commuter train between Tampere and Seinajoki.

I found the train station and went to the ticket cage. I was the only customer. Speaking Finnish, I requested a ticket to Seinäjoki. It turned out the 16.43 train I was supposed to take was only on Fridays. The next train was actually the 18.00.

My clerk was so impressed with my Finnish, she called the other ladies to listen. One of the ladies asked me where I was from.

I told them in Finnish that I was a Rotary Exchange student from Canada, that I was staying in Kotka, that I was off to visit my *kynäystävä* in Seinäjoki.

They wanted to know all about my exchange, and since no one else was in the ticket office I chatted happily with them in Finnish.

When it came time to pay, to my surprise, instead of the forty markka Kirsi had told me it'd cost, the clerk told me I only owed twelve markka.

I repeated the number in surprise, "*Vain kaksitoista?*" *Kaksitoista* sounds nothing like *neljakummenta*, but perhaps Kirsi had said *neljatoista* and I'd confused forty for fourteen?

The clerk nodded and smiled, delighted with my surprise.

I checked the board in the station for the train departure time, and with more than two hours to wait, I set out to explore the area around the train station. With thirty-eight unexpected markka, I could pick up some lunch at a local store, and as I was passing a magazine kioski I saw the most recent issue of the American *Seventeen* magazine. It was about twice what I'd have paid for it home in Canada, but what a treat to share with Kirsi and her two younger sisters!

I bought the magazine, and flipped through it while sitting on a picturesque riverbank, fed gulls, pretty pigeons and some ducks, munching crackers, and sipping on my favourite Jaffa orange pop. I wrote some letters to friends back home and in my journal.

With half an hour to go, I went back to the train station, checked the board. My train left at 18.10 from platform one. It was 17.55, so I hauled my case up the stairs to the platform, I looked for the carriage listed on my ticket, but I couldn't find it.

I saw a conductor and called out, "*Anteeksi! Missä on vaunu?*" Where is this carriage? I showed him my ticket.

His eyes grew huge, "*Tulet! Tulet!* Come!" he cried, waving his arms to follow him, and took off full speed down the stairs and along a passage and up another set of stairs.

Huffing and puffing, my bag bouncing at my side, I arrived beside a train on platform three.

"*Seinäjoen*" he said. To Seinäjoki

I pulled on the door of my assigned carriage.

It didn't open.

I tried again.

The door handle pulled out of my fingers as the train pulled out of the station. I stared after it in astonishment.

I burst into tears.

"Okay. Okay." he said in thickly accented English. "*Tulet.*"

Once again I followed up down the stairs, he took me to the ticket booths and told the clerks that I'd missed the train.

My Finnish had completely deserted me in my distress.

The ladies were crestfallen. "Oh no!" They assured me, it would be all right. They would refund me the price of my ticket.

Quickly, they took my ticket and gave me back twelve markka.

How could I contact my penpal's family and tell them when I was coming?

It was fine. They would call on the station telephone. Did I have the phone number?

I gave them the number and they phoned Kirsi's family. Her younger sister, who spoke only rudimentary English answered the phone. I understood Kirsi was at the station to pick me up from the 16.43 train that didn't run on weekends.

I pulled myself together as best I could, and explained that one train didn't run and I had been aiming for the next train, but that I had missed that one, and now I would be on the 20.10 train.

Kirsi got home, and they put her on the phone. I explained again.

"I'm so sorry I had the wrong time! Don't worry. We'll be there to get you!" Kirsi assured me.

"I'm so sorry that it will be so late!" It would be nearly ten o'clock.

"No, no! It's okay! See you then!"

I hung up the phone and the ladies behind the ticket cages asked if everything was all right now.

"Yes," I smiled, "but now I need another ticket."

"No, no." one smiled. "You don't need a reservation on the later train. There will be lots of room. Your Eurail pass will be sufficient."

"Eurail pass?" I said, looking from one lady to another. "I don't have a Eurail pass."

The ladies looked at one another in dismay.

Bit by bit we worked it out. Because I was a foreigner, they had presumed I had a Eurail pass to travel. When I asked for a *lippu*, a ticket, they presumed I just hadn't known the term *paikkojen varaus,* the correct way to say 'seat reservation.'

I thought about my lunch and my expensive *Seventeen* magazine. "How much is the ticket?"

"*Kolmekymmentanelja markka.*" Thirty-four markka.

I gulped.

I counted my bills onto the counter: ten markka, fifteen markka. Then I began counting the coins.

Sixteen.

Seventeen.

Twenty-one.

Twenty-nine.

With a deep breath I reached thirty-three markka. Tiny coins covered the counter.

I tipped out the tiny bronze pennia coins, each worth a quarter of a Canadian penny.

Thirty-three markka, fifty-two pennia.

Fifty-three.

Sixty-one

Seventy-five

Eighty-seven.

The ladies were holding their breath.

Ninety-six, ninety-seven, ninety-eight, ninety-nine.

Thirty-four markka.

Everyone beamed as they gathered up the coins and printed out my ticket.

I looked into my wallet, counting the remaining coins. I had just thirty-four pennia left—less than one Canadian dime.

"Hyvää matka!" The ladies called. Good journey!

"Don't miss this train," the first lady said with impish grin, writing down the departure time and the platform.

"I won't," I said, and bag in hand, parked myself right on the platform for the two hour wait for the last train to Seinäjoki, thankful for the kindness of strangers and that even the tiniest coins add up.

prompt: foreign coin

Magic on the High Seas

VALERIE DAWN

T HIS STORY EVADED ME for one hundred and
sixty-seven years, sequestered away in a sea chest
of dubious origin, tossed on high seas and seemingly
doomed in fathomless depths. And then the envelope
arrived unexpectedly on my bunk. It was from the pirate
captain of a tall ship, sailor of unknown waters, creative
adventurer, seeker of mysteries, riotous friend of women,
children and faerie folk, instigator of stories and mischief
and wicked fun. I was a proud deckhand on the pirate's
seaworthy clipper, steered into hidden straits away from
the rocks and the doldrums, with a map of magic.

The envelope held in my hands had a slight weight and
bulge, and energy from within pulsed like waves between
my palms. I dug eagerly into the corner of the envelope

and withdrew the treasure, likely from one of the pirate's raids. Ancestors crowded around eager to get glimpses of the contents and impatient to see what I would decipher or discover.

The treasure within was a coin, a '5 PTAS' from some far off unknown foreign land, calling to me. I had numerous souvenir treasures collected on my earlier sea bound adventures. None matched this mysterious one, held earnestly lest it disappear. The Ancestors were restless. There was something they wanted me to discover. I wondered if the coin's origins lay in Turkey or perhaps Greece. With no confirmation of either country, I decided to climb to the crows' nest and broaden my view.

I peered through the mists using my Google spyglass and Spain popped up! I was astounded. The energy of the coin became more urgent. Ancestor Chas emerged right in front of me and said sternly "what took you so long" then he fleetingly, sheepishly grinned. I remembered I was up the mast and quickly scampered down. The name Chas, brother to my great grandfather with a probable birthdate of 1851-2 and the unlikely birthplace of Spain, mysteriously emerged from the mists of old and into the clear light of day on the deck before me.

Chas materialized as REAL as the ship caught the westerly winds and we sailed headlong into the sea of uncertain ancestry together. I took my turn at the helm with Great Uncle Chas by my side to sail the oceans around continents. We discovered Chas was, in fact, Charles Robert and learned of his country, his life as a labourer in the land down under, his marriage and children, too.

His parents emerged as John and Mary from Staffordshire, England and I felt their blood pulsing quickly in my veins.

The magic afoot led me to a long forgotten ship on the high seas, named "Gambia," travelling between Britain and the new colony settlements of Port Phillip and Sydney, Australia. In the Google mists I discovered the times, shipping details and a little of the context of the times. My resources scant, the coin was my compass and Great Uncle Charles my co-conspirator and companion of the high seas. The magic surrounded me and I longed to discover the circumstances of his birth.

There is a piece of wisdom attributed to the North American Indigenous Peoples which states, "I don't know if it happened but I know it's true" and thus I believe this was how it unfolded.

A family set out on board a crowded ship for new lands and a new life. The famines had hit hard. The farmers of the English Midlands rushed to follow the pioneer trail after rumours of gold and an uncrowded land of plenty. In their desperation, tales of hardship, scarcities and primitive or nonexistent shelters awaiting them, were unheard or dismissed by brave men. Heavily pregnant, his mother Mary feared for the trip with an inevitable birthing at sea. Charles would be her third child recorded on the ship's passenger list. It is fair to say she was familiar with the birth process at hand. Her husband, John, stoically disguised his desperate anxiety with the hope of a better life for them all in their new lands down under.

They were held up at the Liverpool dock for some time, awaiting permission for the loaded ship to leave as their vital supplies dwindled with each passing day. The winds dropped and the passengers were unable to leave the ship, which merely languished in the Liverpool harbour awaiting rising winds. Their mood was one of anticlimax mixed with excitement and trepidation for the journey ahead. The ship was the "Gambia" bound for Madeira to take on board more supplies from the Portuguese Island the English had long inhabited. Once they finally set sail under sluggish winds they had to make port early in Spain for additional supplies, although it was rumoured the hull sprung a leak and repairs were urgently needed.

In the middle of a dark night, a storm suddenly brewed and the ship rose and fell higher and lower on its moorings. Passengers were quickly sent ashore, crossing via the precarious gangplank leading to dry ground. It was a terrifying and treacherous crossing for the family of four, the children and Mary in particular.

Once they alighted, the passengers dispersed into whatever meagre lodging could be found. Precious funds were exchanged for local coin. Mary despairing, clutched her belly and was stopped frequently by waves of pain, for she was now in full labour. She fortunately was found by an older, sympathetic, weather-beaten local woman, who bid her with wordless gestures to enter her humble one room abode. John took the children and went seeking shelter elsewhere, vowing to return in the morning.

It was the time just before a red dawning when baby Charles Robert made his way slowly and laboriously into the world wailing loudly to make his voice heard above the gale. The Spanish woman had assisted with the birthing and passed Mary's child to her for Charles to go immediately to breast. She bathed

Mary and made her a bitter herbal tea to which she had added honey and then busied herself making bread and gruel. The spent mother and baby slept.

Mary and baby Charles remained with their good samaritan for over a month while repairs, which could no longer be concealed, progressed on the ship. Mary felt blessed by this stranger's hospitality. Each day she saw her new son growing stronger. Mary was aware they had a gruelling journey ahead, one which was rumoured to often grasp young ones from their parents in the crowded confines of a perilous sea voyage.

When Mary regained her own strength she promptly helped her benefactor with washing, cleaning and meals. She took walks to the market and bought potatoes and onions for them all. She slowly learned rudimentary Spanish but conversation between them was limited to basic survival necessities.

Secretly Mary was terribly homesick and lay awake in the darkness of night until sleep overtook her. She wept silent tears for their families in England they would never see again. She longed for the comfort of John and her other children beside her in the night. Through the night Charles slept on, fortunately never waking beside her, merely stirring as he responded to her pain.

In the days following Charles birth, John and the children visited with them. Mary and John took walks with the babe and talked about their dreams for their future. The children played hopscotch or hide and seek on the cobblestoned streets surrounding the harbour, ducking between piles of supplies and sailors stumbling along the quay. Rainy days were particularly a challenge for all in cramped quarters but they relished their time of freedom on land.

John worked the odd day on the docks, thankfully stretching their financial limitations. On the last day before embarking once more, Mary had one coin left in her purse. It was the meagre yet powerful 5 PTAS coin I held in my hand, supposedly lost at sea by one of the children.

I wondered how the coin made its way into the pirate's treasure chest. Charles considered it inconsequential and left me. The pirate's coin and its magic has bridged time and space for us and for our enduring future ancestral connection. One hundred and sixty-seven years and a pirate's coin later, I, too, am on a ship, this one sailing among the clouds bound for Australia to meet the ancestors of my Great Uncle Chas.

Prompt: Unusual coin

Star Light Star Bright

HOLLY ALFORD

ELENA WAS A TERRIBLY unhappy child. Her natural awkwardness and the relentless teasing she endured from schoolmates assured her she wasn't like the others. Every party that passed without an invitation made her doubt she'd ever have a friend. She was a constant disappointment to her family and never really understood why. She wondered if she would ever fit in, but she still held out hope that things could change. If only she got her ears pierced or gave the perfect gift, she could finally fit in. As time went on, however, Elena started to think that whatever was different about her could only be fixed by divine intervention. Wishes and magic gave her hope.

Elena loved to climb up on the toybox in front of her window and sing the song that gave her the most comfort:

When you want your wish to come true
This is what you have to do
Raise your head up to the sky
And wish upon an evening star
Star Light, Star Bright
The first star I see tonight
I wish I may, I wish I might
Have the wish I wish tonight

Sometimes she would rush to the window to watch the sunset, frantically scanning the skies to be sure she caught the first star that became visible. She was certain that the first star would hold more luck than the second one. Elena would wish for friends. She'd wish for cool clothes. She'd wish her family would love her unconditionally.

As time went on, though, Elena's belief that things could get better faded. She doubted that any of her wishes would ever come true. Life beat the magic out of her. Friendships were lost over trivial arguments. Instead of being surrounded by a loving family she became estranged from the only family she knew. Life became one hit after another. She stopped scanning the stars every night and fell into a bitter life of desperation.

Even through the darkness, small things would appear to remind Elena of that song, that youthful hope, that somewhere out there someone would be able to grant her secret wishes. In her most desperate moments, a treasured song would play while she walked through a store. During a tearful night, a message would arrive from a long-lost friend. These synchronicities appeared when she could least see any way to keep going. It was like the universe wanted to save her from complete hopelessness. This would help for a little while and, like in her youth, she would watch the sky and recite her song but the magic always wore off far too quickly.

It wasn't until she was much older, more cynical, but still wanting her life to be different, that a simple object arrived, sparking an amazing epiphany. She was opening a package and out fell an unexpected item, a bookmark. On it were the words, "Star light, Star bright." Elena gazed at it in awe. She was reminded of her song and within moments, just like magic, she finally realized the song's hidden secret.

Like a bookmark reminds her where she is in the story she is reading, Elena realized the stars are there to remind her of where she is in the story of the universe. She understood, in this moment of clarity, that the universe had been ticking along since well before she was born, and it had conspired to put her in just the place she was meant to be at every point in her life. There was nothing wrong with her, she had always been right where she needed to be.

A flood of relief came over her knowing she could stop fighting against the universe and simply have faith in her song and the stars that gave her joy when she was young. It had never been about granting a material wish. The song had been telling her all along that if she would just look up and gaze at the miracle of the stars, she would feel peace in her soul; a peace that surpassed any peace that could be gained by the granting of a single wish. The song's secret was that contemplating the universe could put any problem into perspective and, in that process, she was guaranteed to get her wish of feeling better. That night

Elena gazed up at the stars and sang the Star Light Star Bright song. She could feel the child in her smile and she felt her own glow as she smiled back.

—ele—

Prompt: book mark

Lost Watch

SHAWN L. BIRD

T HE WATCH ARRIVED UNEXPECTEDLY with a box
of writing prompts. She had unwrapped the tissue
and stared at it for a long time, pondering serendipity,
synchronicity, and the nature of the world. It was a
well-worn watch, gold finish rubbed off the band and face.
It was never going to work again.

She'd unwrapped the same watch at Christmas, the year
she was fifteen. "This was expensive," her mother had said.
"We expect you to look after it." It was stylish, mature. She
was proud and glad of their trust. She volunteered at the
hospital, and at first she'd asked for a watch like the nurses
wore on their chests, numbers mounted upside down so
just a tip of the chin revealed the time, and the wrists were
bare for the interminable washing. But by the end of the

year she was fourteen, she knew that despite a love for Candystriping at the hospital, she was never going to be a nurse, and she'd altered her Christmas list to "a nice wristwatch." Her new watch was perfect. She wore it to school every day and felt grown up.

In February, the school production was mounted at the local theatre. Each performance she removed earrings, necklace, and watch. She put them into a Crown Royal bag she drew closed and looped the strings over the hanger with her street clothes when she put on her costume. After the third performance, her watch wasn't in the bag. She appealed to the director, spread word among the other students, begged for her Christmas watch back. Amid the close family atmosphere of a theatrical production, she'd been betrayed. The joy of the show was tainted. Her parents' faith in her responsibility was tarnished. With an ache in her throat and tears in her eyes, she had to tell them her watch had been stolen. Her mother scowled. Her father sighed. They called the school, complained to the administration and the drama teacher. Everyone looked oh so sympathetic as they shrugged. Just as when her gym strip and new runners had been stolen from her locker the year before, there was nothing they could do. Thieves remained hidden. "It's too bad," everyone said. "We're so sorry that happened," they said. But the watch was gone. She held her grief in her heart and thought, someday.

She hadn't seen the watch for forty years.

But here it is again. Worn out and broken. It's useless, except as a reminder: time moves along. The small and great tragedies of our life are only moments of shadow. Karma will bring back what is meant to be.

She holds in her hand a worn gold watch that shows the right time twice a day, and smiles.

—*ele*—

prompt: broken watch

Shatter

COREENA McBURNIE

S MASH. ANOTHER DISH HIT the wall with a satisfying slam. Shards of tasteful, flower patterned, gold trimmed plate flew across the garage. Crash. An elegant teacup followed, adding to the substantial pile of destruction. With every shattered piece of dishware, Jane felt a weight lift off her shoulders. She took a deep breath and winged a bowl at the wall.

"What the hell is going on?", Olivia yelled from behind her.

"Oh, hi dear." Jane turned to her daughter and raised the goggles from her eyes. "If you're going to stay, you should grab the other pair of goggles from the bench."

"Mom, what are you doing? Have you completely lost your mind?" Olivia made no move toward the bench and the goggles but put her hands on her hips and furrowed her brow.

"Just the opposite," replied her mother. "Stand back, dear." Jane repositioned her goggles and picked up a dessert plate from the box at her feet, turned, and hurled it at the wall. It felt so satisfying. She knew her daughter would benefit from throwing a few plates, though she never would do something so unseemly, at least not until she had a few more years under her belt. After all, it had taken Jane until she was nearly sixty to have the courage.

"Mom, stop it. Your dishes. You can't break them like that." Panic rose in Olivia's voice.

Jane shrugged. "Why not? I've never really liked them." She winged a dinner plate at the wall. "It's cathartic."

"But they're your dishes!"

"Exactly." Crash went a serving platter.

"What will the neighbours think? You can hear the crashing from down the block!"

Jane laughed. "They'll probably think I'm off my rocker."

Olivia turned away, pulled out her phone, and hit a number in her contact list. Her shoulders tensed as another plate shattered against the wall.

"Troy, its Olivia." Crash. "Listen, can you come over right away? Mom's going crazy. She's in the garage smashing the plates and she won't stop. I don't know what's wrong, but she won't listen to reason." Crash. "Thanks. See you in five."

Olivia put her phone away and turned to her mother. "Troy will be here in a few minutes. Why don't we go inside and we can talk about this."

"When I'm done, dear."

Olivia rolled her eyes and walked to the end of the driveway to wait for her brother while nervously eyeing her clearly mad mother.

Whoosh. Smash. Whoosh. Smash.

Troy pulled up and raced into the garage just as Jane flung the last of the tableware at the garage wall, which now joined a matched set of shards on the garage floor.

"What the…?" Troy laughed. "Mom? What's going on? Are you alright?"

"No, she is clearly not alright," said Olivia, standing next to her brother. "She said she doesn't like the dishes. And her solution? Instead of getting new ones like any sane person would do, she's throwing them against the wall. She must be having a breakdown."

"Actually, I'm seeing things very clearly," said Jane. "Come in for something to drink? I'll clean this up later."

Troy looked from his mom to his sister and stifled a snicker, nodding and following Jane into the house. Olivia stomped after them.

"I think tea is out," said Jane, rummaging around in the pantry, "no cups. But I have some nice Irish Whiskey and jam jars." She put three jars on the counter and poured out generous servings over ice.

"We don't want whiskey out of jam jars in the middle of the day, mom," exclaimed Olivia.

"Speak for yourself," said Troy, taking a sip. "Smooth."

"It's the good stuff," said Jane, motioning to the table.

Olivia made a point of not touching her drink as she harumphed into her chair. "What's gotten into you? Dad would be mad."

Jane took a sip of her whiskey and shook her head. "He hated those dishes more than I did. He'd be proud of me. I'm sure he's looking down on us and having a great laugh."

"This is not funny," pointed out Olivia. "I think you need help."

"Only in cleaning up," said Jane. She put her jar on the table and took in her two grown children. Her pride and joy. Olivia, twenty-four, confident, a successful financial planner who liked an even keel. Troy, twenty-one, almost done nursing school, a little more prone to rocking the boat. Their faces were so young and dewy, like dappled sunshine on a late spring day. They were the light of her life, the best things her and Andrew did. She missed him so much every day that it hurt.

Jane, on the other hand, had a face like a crumpled piece of paper that she had tried, rather unsuccessfully, to smooth out. Each line, each wrinkle, each crease spoke to her years of experience, her joys and sorrows, her years under the sun. The wrinkles and the greying hair put her into a different category, one which she wasn't sure she was ready for, one that made her even more invisible than normal, and all at a time when she wasn't willing to put up with anyone's bullshit anymore.

"Bit strange to smash up the dishes when you could have just given them to the charity shop," confirmed Troy. "But whatever."

"It was liberating," said Jane. "But while you're both here, I have something to talk to you about." Jane took a Dutch courage swig of her drink. "I'm going to sell the house."

Both Olivia's and Troy's jaws dropped. Jane raised her hand to stop the tirade she knew was coming. "I've been thinking about it for awhile. I don't need a whole, big house anymore. And there are things I'd rather be doing than maintenance all the time. I know this will be hard on you, after all, this is where you grew up and there are so many memories here. Your father, your childhood, all the good times. But it's time."

"That makes sense," said Olivia, with a sigh.

"Yeah," agreed Troy. "Still kind of hard though."

"Yes. For me too. I'm not doing this lightly. And you two can have anything you want." Jane waved her arm around.

Olivia got up and retrieved her glass of whiskey from the counter, visibly more relaxed. This was all just a reaction to making a big decision. They could deal with this. "Where will you move to? There are some great communities for people your age. Lots of activities. Low maintenance. Good security. I have a realtor friend who can set up some condo viewings."

"Actually, I've already found a place. It just fell into my lap," said Jane, smiling into her jam jar.

"Where?" asked Troy.

"It's a little cottage on the edge of town. Nice and quiet. I can have wildflowers instead of a lawn."

"You've got to be kidding me," said Olivia, slamming her jar on the table.

"Why?" asked Jane. "Wait until you see it, it's lovely. And there's a spare room if you ever want to stay."

"Because it doesn't make sense," huffed Olivia. "If you move to a condo then we wouldn't have to worry about you, there'd be people around. But you want to move into an isolated cottage by yourself instead. You're being selfish."

"I'm sorry you feel that way, but you don't have to worry about me," said Jane. "And yes, I know I'm being selfish, but I want to live somewhere with a bit of peace and quiet, at least for awhile."

"Yes, we do have to worry, especially if today is anything to go by," said Olivia, pointing with her jar in the direction of the garage.

"Haven't you ever wanted to smash things?" asked Jane. "Just to hear them shatter? There was so much expectation when your father and I received those dishes. They were a lovely gift. Pretty and practical. They weren't our taste, but it felt silly to spend the money to replace them. And they did their job. But I'm ready for something new now."

"There's nothing wrong with doing what you're supposed to," said Olivia defensively.

Jane put her hand over Olivia's. "Nothing at all. And I wouldn't change things for the world. Except maybe that your father was still here. But I want a change now. I want to do things for other reasons than because I'm supposed to. I'm tired of waiting for permission to do things. I'm taking things into my own hands."

Olivia looked to her brother. "You're being awfully quiet. What do you think of all this?"

Troy shrugged. "If it's what mom wants, it sounds like she's thought this through."

Olivia sat back in her chair. "So, moving to a cottage will give you the change you want?"

Jane took a deep breath. Society wanted her to shuffle away into a gated community where they wouldn't have to look at her aging face and be reminded of their own race toward the inevitable, but, quite frankly, she was done smoothing things over. Her face was a map of creases and so was her attitude, crumpled like a piece of paper with dark, smeared words, and ready to throw at the next person who tried to pigeonhole her. She was tired of crumpling the paper of herself to fit into some societal box. She was ready to pull the paper out, open it, and show off what was written there. The ebbing and flowing tides of life had smudged many of the words, making them hard to read, making her hard to read. "Yes, it will, but I'm also going travelling." She might as well rip the bandaid off and get it all out in the open.

Olivia put her head in her hands. "Something tells me you're not going on a nice, sensible cruise with a friend."

"No, I am not," said Jane. "First, I'm visiting Scotland to tour the Highlands, then I'm popping up to Iceland for a charity trek around the volcanos. We're raising money for The Women's Hospital."

Jane looked at her children. Olivia looked like she might start to boil over. Troy had a puppy dog grin on his face.

"Wow," said Troy. "Castles and volcanoes, it sounds amazing. Remember that volcano project I did as a kid? I've always wanted to see a real volcano."

Jane grinned like a kid on Christmas morning. "I met a group of women online from all across the country. We're going to meet in Iceland in a few months. I've already started training."

"I don't even know what to say," said Olivia evenly into her now empty mason jar. "An online group. Do you even hear yourself? You sound like you're having a midlife crisis. You'd never be acting so irresponsibly if Dad were still here. I don't even know you anymore." Olivia's head was spinning from the news, her mother's uncharacteristic behaviour, and the whiskey.

"I've spent my whole life waiting for permission to do things and I need to change that. For me. But I'll always be there for you and your brother."

"I don't get it. You've got a life here. Us, friends, your job. Can't you just take up a new hobby? Go on a cruise? Do you have to smash dishes and walk around Icelandic volcanos? Nobody in their right bloody mind pops up to Iceland!" Olivia stood up, grabbed her now empty jam jar and stared into it for a long moment, then swung her arm back and threw it at the kitchen wall. Smash. Glass shards flew across the room.

Stunned silence filled the room, followed by the sound of Jane laughing so hard she had to wipe tears from her eyes.

Olivia stared at the broken jar. "What have I done?" She stared wide-eyed at her mother.

Jane got up and put her arm around her daughter, who had devolved into nervous giggles. Troy had his hand over his mouth trying to supress his laughter.

"Cathartic, isn't it?" said Jane.

Prompts: crumpled paper and Paint Chip Poetry

Watches and Time

VALERIE DAWN

I RAISED THE LID on the magic box. There lay an old strapless ladies wrist watch, transporting me instantaneously to my mother. In that moment as I peered into the box, Mum's gold watch, though band-less, belonged to me. I held it tenderly in my hand as I marvelled and turned it over and over between my fingers in a boundary-less time warp. It felt so precious in its solid smoothness. The significance of watches, their treasured intergenerational gifted place in an earlier time, blended and rippled through my digital reality of keepsake losses. In my later years I had entered into a disposable, technological time of consumerism.

I shuddered and returned to my mother's watch firmly grasped between my fingers. I recalled the gold bracelet styled band and the concertinaed clasp. I could see my Mum donning the watch and securing the clasp then adjusting it on her wrist. I was lost in the memory of a treasured ritual of adornment and practicality which suddenly gained significance through recollection and this palpable connection. I remembered too how Mum had given me her earlier watch. It was a tiny, thin, silver rectangular watch face with a narrow, well worn black leather strap. It was gifted to her by her parents for her fourteenth birthday.

I then recalled my own marcasite dream watch, a present from my parents for passing my Junior State Examination at the end of Junior High School. Dad had bought me the watch the day before the results were known, an out of character expensive gift. Meanwhile Mum and I had paced and waited anxiously at home for the results, published in the Western Australian newspaper for all to see. We waited and circled the phone. My Auntie Vi would call with the results from the city before the newspaper was available for circulation in the country.

I passed all nine examinations. I remember being outraged because Dad procured the watch before he had knowledge of the results. I didn't like his bold expectation and belief I couldn't fail. I didn't appreciate his extreme confidence in my academic abilities. Dad had exacting standards in everything which no one met, especially himself I suspect. Looking back across decades I concede to his confidence in me. I'm less contorted by thoughts of success or failure these days.

Time has taught me the hard way at times. I'm not the best wife, mother, grandmother, nurse, teacher, healer, writer, etc. I no longer feel the need to be the best everything to be a worthwhile person. I only feel compelled to be the best me, warts and all. Therein lies personal peace and freedom when I unashamedly surrender to the possibility of so-called failure.

A day or two passes. I look again at the watch face in my hand. My eyes widen. The watch today is round! It's clearly not my mother's although I'd have sworn to it when I first saw and held it. Today I know it's definitely not my mother's. My sister has Mum's gold watch which adorned her wrist most of her life; a gift from Dad. I know my mother's watch had a rectangular face, not round. How could I have been so mistaken? Was it magic? I wonder when I'm gone, how my daughters will connect across time with me?

Today my own daughters don't wear heirloom or gifted watches. Although both in health care, my nursing watches have long since vanished. Cell phones have superseded watches. Cell phone replacement has become compulsory every few years by the inevitable disposable consumerism with an ever-increasing demand for technological advancement. Time is warped and distorted in new ways and possessions are numerous and transitory and no longer tell our stories of old.

We have lost a part of ourselves in the process. We can unintentionally speed past our own history many times in one lifetime. Generations of technology can erode connections through digital surrogates, loss of human-to-human contact and loss of the gift of scarcity. It's unlikely anyone will hold an old cell and remember its connection to me or another through its feel or blank screen. If however someone should walk in the woods and touch a tree, or lay on their back watching clouds or crows, or find an iPhone photo of our shared joys, I hope then they fall into a time warp and remember the love we once held between us. I hope they'll take time to be wild, to connect to the earth as I have done.

Time and travels shift perceptions of many things. May we use them as a starting point for recording our legacy. May our stories and those of our ancestors be honoured and hold wisdom for those we love who come after us. May they follow us backwards through memory, and forwards by the legacy and values gifted into their own times.

Prompt: watch

What Old Men Carry

MARY JORDAN

T RAVELLING RECENTLY, I FOUND myself chatting with an old gent on the pier in Stornoway, a small town in the Outer Hebrides of Northern Scotland. He was getting out of his car with a little dog who was obviously excited for his walkabout. Dogs are always a great icebreaker to connect into conversation with strangers. We were soon hearing Douggie's history from this engaging man with twinkling eyes and an obvious gift for spinning yarns.

Douggie, it seems, was not from the Islands and his benefactor had travelled to the South of England to retrieve this little terrier. His name was Diego, we were told with a chuckle, but that would never do. No self-respecting Highland dog could have a name like Diego.

"Far too shameful," he chortled, "Douggie would be quite embarrassed." And so, Diego soon became Douggie. He and Douggie did very well we were assured.

"He insists on walks and I am happy to oblige," he smiled, "We get on very well".

The conversation shifted to the changes in Stornoway over the years. He waved his hand toward the harbour filled with sail boats and fishing boats. On closer inspection, we were aware that a good deal of them were pleasure boats. When he was a boy, the old man told us, the harbour was filled with fishing boats and he and the lads would filch what they could, string them through their gills and run them home. There was a smile on his face at the memories. A picture emerged of a poor family with a bevy of kids and an overworked mother bent with the task of feeding and managing her unruly lot.

He was well dressed in a fine Harris Tweed jacket and a jaunty flat cap popular in Scotland. Learning that The Hebrides was home, I envisioned that he must have been a merchant, a lawyer or man of some means. We enquired what his work had been. His demeanour shifted noticeably, and a shadow crossed his face revealing a hint of sadness and regret.

"Well," he began, his brogue becoming softer; "that's difficult," he said. "If you were to tell me you were a teacher, I would know exactly what you did or if you were to say you were a fireman or a farmer, I would know what you did. Well," he said looking at us seriously, as though he were about to make a confession, "I was a soldier."

An old man but hardly the age of a World War II Vet, he mentioned deployment in places like Cypress, Malaysia,

Indonesia and Dhofar. The Brits have played their part in the blood baths of the later half of the 20th Century. He continued with his story.

"I was in many places and I saw a lot but I can't speak about those things," he said, "They aren't experiences you talk about with your family at the dinner table." My friend interjected with some words of understanding about his experiences. He looked at her and said, "And neither can I talk about the things I did." The tears began to cradle in his eyes. We turned to a moment of silence, acknowledging the price of war and the burdens that old men carry.

His attention turned again to Douggie, who had been put in the car while he took time for conversation. We knew in the course of our conversation that he and Douggie lived alone. And that, while they did very well, he had dipped us into his loneliness.

"Well," he said, surfacing from the shadows of his memories, "Douggie is getting impatient for his walk. We'd best get on".

***

prompt: haunted

The Ring

COREENA MCBURNIE

SUNDAY
    Adam sat on the couch watching TV, three empty beer bottles already on the coffee table next to his feet, another, almost empty in his hand, and Luna, a grey tabby cat, curled up on a cushion next to him. An ad came on, the music had a Middle Eastern flair. The cat's ears twitched.

"Ancient Egyptian Exhibit coming to the museum. Starts next month and will run through the summer," the TV blared.

Luna raised her head and fixed her eyes on the TV. Adam made for the remote control, but she swatted his hand away and hissed, meowing strangely. If he didn't know any better, he'd say the cat was speaking to him. He shook his head, put down his beer, and followed the cat's gaze to the commercial about the museum exhibit.

"Looks pretty great, eh?" said Adam. "I used to love all that ancient Egyptian stuff and mummies when I was a kid."

Luna raised her eyebrows in distain.

The camera on the commercial panned a display of ancient Egyptian jewelry and Luna lunged for the screen, her paw touching a ring with a lioness head. Adam paused the TV and Luna nodded, her paw glued to the screen as she looked longingly at the ring.

Adam shook his head. This behaviour was strange, even for his pampered housecat. Adam made a move to unpause the TV and Luna lunged at him.

"Woah, girl. I guess you like the ring?"

Luna nodded and meowed strangely again.

"Are you trying to tell me something?"

Luna nodded and gave Adam a withering look. Then her eyes turned to the smart home speaker. She pounced on it, turning it on.

"Hey, what the..." Before Adam could finish his sentence, Luna turned and hissed at him, baring her teeth. Adam backed away. "I think I've had too much to drink," he mumbled.

After a few more taps with her nose, Luna meowed into the speaker.

"Human servant, do you understand me now?" said the robotic voice.

Adam's eyes popped open and his jaw dropped. "This can't be right. Do I hear what I think I'm hearing?"

Meow. "Yes. I'm talking to you, servant. I want my ring back."

Adam picked up the speaker and saw that it was translating from Ancient Egyptian. "You speak Egyptian?"

Luna sat up as straight as she could and gave Adam her most regal look. "I most certainly do. It is my language as Bastet, Goddess of the Home and Childbirth. I am also called Eye of the Moon, so Luna is an acceptable name. Barely. I want you to get that ring for me."

"Um, wow. This is a lot to take in. I'm not sure I understand."

Meow. "What words do you not understand? Have I not made myself clear, peon?" Luna licked her paw.

"You're a cat. How can you be talking? How can I understand you? You can't be an Ancient Egyptian goddess. Those are just myths."

If looks could kill, Adam would be dead. *Meow.* "You can understand me because of your speaker. It is translating my words for you. Is that clear?"

"I guess so." Adam scratched his head.

"And I am Bastet. Our being has been passed down through the millennia. We are not myth."

"You're a goddess, for real?"

"Yes, and as such, I demand that ring. It is mine and I would like it returned."

"But, it's in a museum. I can't just take it."

Luna slammed her paw on the table, rattling the empty beer bottles. "That is not acceptable. I require the ring. You see the insignia on it marking it as mine? The lioness? I need it. I was once buried with this ring."

"Why do you want it?"

"You dare to question me? You are here only to serve me. Now execute my will."

Adam put down his beer. He definitely had drunk too much. The best thing he could do would be to diffuse this situation and get some sleep. "I can see this is really important to you. How about this? I sleep on it and we'll talk about it in the morning."

"Figure it out." Luna turned longingly to the screen. "I need that ring. In the meantime, I require more tuna. I don't know why you don't give me more tuna as I clearly enjoy it." She jumped onto the pillow on the couch, curled up, and fell asleep.

Adam shook his head, hoping this would make sense in the morning.

Monday

Adam woke up to Luna swatting his face and meowing the strange meow again. "It's too early for this."

Meow. "Have you come up with a plan yet, human servant?"

Adam bolted upright in bed and rubbed his eyes. Luna had turned on his smart speaker in his bedroom. "I must still be dreaming."

"Not this again. I explained everything last night. I expected you to have a plan by now, human."

"I need coffee." Adam swung his legs out of bed and made his way to the kitchen.

Luna followed. *Meow.* "What is the plan?"

"I don't have one."

"Why not?"

"Because this whole thing is crazy. I must be losing it. Working too hard."

"Hardly. You do the bare minimum. You live in this measly apartment. My ancestors lived in luxury. Do better and get me my ring."

Adam put his head in his hands. "This can't be real."

"I assure you that it is. Where is my breakfast? Tuna, remember?"

Adam rummaged around the cupboards and found a tin of tuna, opened it, and dumped it into a bowl.

"Don't forget the ring," Luna commanded as she began to eat.

An hour later, Adam sat at his desk in the large, open plan office where he worked as a reporter for the local paper. He searched the museum on his computer, trying to find out more about the exhibit. What was he thinking? He couldn't rob a museum! Cats can't talk and his cute little grey tabby was not an Egyptian goddess.

Adam sat back. Was he really considering robbing a museum to appease his cat when he was probably having a psychotic break? That certainly made more sense than Luna being Bastet. He made a note to pick up more tuna on the way home.

"Look at you, checking out local culture," June peered at the computer screen over his shoulder.

Adam perked up. "I love Ancient Egypt. I can't believe this exhibit is coming to town. I can hardly wait to see it. Are you covering this?"

"Yeah. There's a preview for reporters next week."

This was his chance. "Really? That would be amazing. I'm so jealous."

"Well, come then," said Jane. "There's a whole wine and cheese schmooze fest thing. Private tour. You can be my plus one."

Adam sat back. It couldn't be this easy. "Are you sure? Don't tease me."

"It will be fun to have company and I'll bet you scrub up well." June winked.

"Sure, sounds great. Text me the details?"

June nodded and ran off to talk to someone else. He was going to be in the gallery, now all he had to do was figure out a way to steal the ring. No problem. Ugh.

Adam returned home that night with printouts about the museum and the upcoming exhibit.

Meow, demanded Luna as he entered.

"Give me a minute," Adam said, turning on the translation app and unloading his tuna onto the counter.

"Do you have the ring?"

"No, of course not. The exhibit isn't even open yet!"

Meow. "But I told you I want it."

"Yes, and I'm working on it. I've arranged to be at a special preview showing for reporters in a few days. But I still don't see how I'm going to pull this off."

"That is not my problem, peasant. My concern is only with the return of my ring."

"I got you some tuna."

Luna twitched her nose, stretched out her glorious leg to groom it, then ate her tuna.

Tuesday

Adam woke up to Luna swatting his nose, demanding to know where the ring was and why the tuna bowl was empty. Adam sat up in bed, his bleary eyes taking in the time, 3:07 am.

"What the hell, Luna!" he grumbled.

"I want my ring, puny human," mewed Luna.

Adam pulled himself out of bed and opened a can of tuna.

Work wasn't much better and Adam felt like he was sleep walking through the whole day. He fell asleep interviewing someone for an article, then got yelled at by his boss. The article he was working on got sent back three times for mistakes. He bought a bottle of whiskey along with the tuna on the way home.

That night at home, the papers he had piled up on the table were all over the floor, some shredded, others simply with teeth marks. As he salvaged what he could, Luna simply meowed, "I want my ring," before curling up on the couch to take a well-deserved nap.

Wednesday

Adam woke up late for work and put his foot into his shoe only to find that Luna had thrown up a hairball into it. He had to resist the temptation to throw the shoe at the cat and instead balled up his sock and threw it across the room to deal with later. At work, he sat down to his computer and searched replica ancient Egyptian rings. He found a good quality gold one that looked close enough to the one from the exhibit and put a rush order on it. His credit card would not thank him for this. He prayed this would appease his diminutive lioness.

Thursday

Thursday morning was uneventful until Adam tried to put on his shoes for work only to find the shoelaces had been chewed off and the limp remains sat taunting him on the floor.

"Damn, Luna!" he exclaimed.

Meow. "You are taking too long getting my ring. I grow weary of the delays. Do you know what would have happened to any servant who took this long to do my bidding back when I was revered properly? He would have been flogged. You should be flogged."

"I'm doing my best and you chewing my shoelaces and ripping up my work only makes it harder to get your damn ring."

"Did I ask for excuses?"

At work Adam checked the tracking on the replica ring every hour. When he got home, he found that Luna had swatted the kitty litter all over the floor and it took everything for Adam not to cry. He couldn't live like this. But he wouldn't have to for much longer. The ring would arrive the next day and that would be that. So long as he kept Luna fed with tuna.

Friday

Adam came home early from work to check the mailbox. The ring arrived and, as far as Adam could tell, it was perfect. It was heavy, gold, and had a lioness on it. He tossed the box away and ran up to his apartment to show Luna. He threw open the door and held out the ring like an anxious suitor. Toilet paper was strewn across the apartment. Never mind, he thought. This will all be over soon.

"What's this piece of tat?" Luna asked.

"It's your ring," said Adam.

Luna pushed it with her nose. "No, this is not my ring. How dare you try to fob me off with this inferior rubbish. Do you think I'm a fool?"

"No, of course not," Adam back peddled. "But it is made of gold and to the same specifications as the original. I thought it might, you know, do."

Meow. "Well, you pea brained human, it will not do. It is not my ring. I demand my ring. What's taking you so long? You are being most ineffectual." Luna walked slowly over to the end table, jumped up, and, while staring at Adam, knocked over the lamp.

"No," Adam yelled, too late as the lamp smashed on the floor. "What do you think you're doing?"

"Being this ineffectual would have earned a servant the loss of a hand back in my heyday."

"Tomorrow," said Adam. "I'm going to the exhibit tomorrow."

Luna flicked her tail and went off for a nap, clearly exhausted from dealing with her lowly human. Adam took the ring and examined it. It was gorgeous. Damn cat. He tucked it into his sock drawer for safe keeping, hoping beyond hope that there would be an opportunity to switch it for the original. He popped open a beer and opened his research folder on the gallery and the exhibit on his laptop. He had to learn every detail he could. Lack of sleep was getting to him, as Luna exerted more and more pressure.

Saturday

Finally, the day of the exhibit preview arrived. Adam dressed in his best clothes and hid the fake ring in the lining of his jacket. He met June outside the museum and together they climbed the stairs, his heart racing faster with each step. June walked by his side, chatting away obliviously. At the top of the stairs, Adam breathed to calm himself, reminding himself of his plan, that this would all work out, that he'd make the tiny Ancient Egyptian Goddess Bastet very happy and that he would live a happy life because of it. He could do this. He had a lioness goddess on his side, after all.

Adam opened the door for June and they stepped into the gallery, which had been decorated in an Egyptian theme for the event. There was a bar set up on the side and people were mingling.

"Do you want a drink?" asked June.

"Um, maybe just a soda water for now," said Adam, wanting to keep a clear head. That last thing he needed was to dull his senses.

"I didn't take you for a teetotaller," said June.

"I'm just so excited to be here, I don't want to miss anything." Adam flashed June a smile.

Adam checked his watch every five minutes through the speeches and drinks until it was finally time for the actual tour. This was it. They were led through several rooms of mummies and grave goods while the curator explained the history and significance of what they were seeing. Adam lamented that he was too preoccupied to enjoy the tour.

Finally, they entered a room with some jewelry and Adam's heart raced.

"Relax," said June beside him. "This is meant to be fun."

Adam forced a smile. "My inner ten-year-old is overwhelmed, that's all."

The curator explained that the glass was removed from some of the exhibits for better photography for the reporters and Adam couldn't believe his luck. All of the precious gold jewelry was on full display. He simply needed to find the correct ring and swap it for the replica, which he was now clutching in his pocket. No problem. Right. He wiped his sweaty palms on his trousers as unobtrusively as he could.

Adam wandered away from June and frantically searched the cases while trying to appear casual. He spotted it in the third case. It was unmistakable. Adam tried to look nonchalant as he made his way over to the case. He pulled his hand out of his pocket, fake ring tucked inside.

"Gorgeous, aren't they?" asked June.

Adam nearly jumped out of his skin. "Y-Y-Yes. Very nice. So detailed."

"Yes, look at the lion on this one," said June, pointing to the very ring Adam was trying to steal. "Unbelievable craftsmanship." June framed the ring in her camera and took a picture. "Having fun?"

"Absolutely. This is a dream come true," said Adam.

June moved onto the next case. Adam took a quick look around. No one appeared to be looking at him. Before he could change his mind, he reached over and swapped the rings. He stood there, stunned with what he'd just done, waiting for the alarms to go off or for someone to shout at him. Nothing happened so he wandered to the next display as normally as he could with his heart racing at dangerous speeds.

The rest of the night was an anxious blur of fear and relief. As soon as he could, Adam said his goodbyes and raced out of the museum to his car. He'd done it. He had the ring.

Adam came home to find his kitchen cupboards emptied all over the floor, but simply kicked the containers aside as he called out for Luna.

"I did it, Luna, I have the ring!" Adam exclaimed.

Luna uncurled herself and stretched before sauntering over to Adam who was crouching down with a big grin on his face and holding out the ring. The diminutive lioness smelled the ring then nodded.

Meow. "Finally, you have succeeded," the robotic speaker voice affirmed.

Not knowing what else to do, Adam put the ring down in front of the cat, who proceeded to paw at it, sending it across the room, then pouncing on it. This went on for at least five minutes as Adam watched, stunned that Luna would treat such an important artifact as a toy, but too scared to say anything. Then, with a good swat, the ring spun its way under the couch. Luna crouched down to see where it had gone, tried to paw at it, but when she couldn't reach it, jumped on the couch, yawned, and curled up into a ball for a nap.

Adam sat on the couch next to Luna, incredulous. "Is that it?"

Meow. "You're interrupting my nap."

Prompts: random choices from Writerly Spell Cards: a frantic reporter, a cat that speaks Egyptian, a remote control, comedy

The Gloria Theatre

SHANNON LALONDE

WHEN I WAS YOUNG, I was the talk of the town. People lived, died, wept, lied, whispered and murmured. They were entranced, enthralled, enraged. Took flight, transformed, and were taken away to marvelous places, all because of me.

Without me there would have been no shrieks of delight, raucous applause, gasps of awe, amazement, wonder, and even, occasionally, fear.

Without me there would not have been hundreds, possibly thousands of curtain calls.

But alas, the final curtain call broke my heart and all the hearts of those that worked within me.

The warm lights are a memory now. I sometimes feel cold, alone and forgotten.

Now, sounds will occasionally creep inside me. Not the sounds the people intentionally made, but wonderful melodies none-the-less. One heavenly tone can build upon the other like the beautiful symphonic music I embraced years ago. The rise and fall of the sweet and natural composition fill my lungs and I feel like I can truly breathe once again.

The new music within can start easily enough. The wind rattles a pane of glass, a breeze whistles through a crack – rocking the ropes still hanging on the main stage curtain rod, adding a gentle hum to the whistling tune. The tattered rope tassels gently sweep the floor and whisper to the others to join the dance. If the wind outside is strong enough, some of it slips inside – then the ropes and rods swing and sway to create a glorious song and dance that would rival any performance the people used to do, when I was young.

I can still picture the performers dancing and swirling around the stage. The blush on the women's cheeks. The hems of their dresses would brush and kiss the floor. The men would smile as they confidently held their partners, and guided them through astounding maneuvers, never missing a beat of the music, or a well-placed step on the floor. When the music at the end of an evening finally stopped, the performers would freeze in place, their costumes swayed and magically did not stop until the last musical note faded into silence. The thunderous sound of applause would rise and then fall. The audience would leave, and eventually the performers would too. The sound of their chattering and shoes on the floor always filled my heart. I didn't mind the lights going out or hearing the key turn in the big red door. I knew they would come back again.

But then something happened. Slowly. They didn't come back as often. The performers or the audience. The auditorium chairs did not fill like they used to.

One cool evening, the man who used to sing my name until it echoed in the rafters, locked the big red door, rested his hand on my faded red door, and whispered "I'm sorry, Gloria", then left.

I don't know why all the people had to leave and not return, but they never came back.

In the beginning, in my youth, life seemed so much simpler. I had no idea what I was to become. Long wooden boards were pieced together with thick iron nails to form what became my tall walls. Openings where windows and two grand doors would be, were carved out from my sides to allow warm sunshine and, eventually, people to flood in. Beautiful, thick, clear panes of glass were placed in the window spaces. Light shone through them, and waves of sunshine would dance across the walls and floors. Two strong, beautiful red-stained doors were bolted in place at the front of me. They were often swung open to welcome the world inside. A grand wooden roof was eventually placed on top of me to keep out the wind and the rain.

It's funny how I welcome the wind now.

There were days when the sound of hammers and saws and people talking was almost deafening. The smell of sweet sawdust, varnish and paint was exhilarating. Balconies, stairs, chairs, and floors were made and placed within my walls. Strange new lights were installed on my walls, and became guides for people as they moved further into my darkened auditorium.

I was enthralled by the cluster of small dazzling lights hanging from my ceiling. They shone like the stars I remembered seeing flicker in the darkness before my roof was in place. My ceiling became as enticing as the night sky.

A second floor with several steps was placed towards the back of me. I didn't understand why I needed the new floor, but I had faith that everything was in its place for a reason.

One bright and sunny morning, I heard a singular strong and masculine voice say the second floor was to be the grand stage. The next part of his conversation changed my life. He pointed at the stage and said, "This is where the magic will happen." Magic? A part of me? I had no idea what the word meant, but it sounded perfectly - enchanting. A melodic feminine voice rang out from the big red doorway and exclaimed "She's beautiful! No. She's glorious!".

I still was not sure what the stage inside me was, or what beautiful meant, but I knew I would love whatever was to become of me.

Finally, the hammering, drilling, sawing, painting and gluing stopped. The smell of wood, paint and people faded. Everything was dark and quiet for what seemed like an eternity. One joyous day the big doors swung open, and the beautiful Spring air came rushing in. The breeze swept down the aisles, over the chairs and up onto the stage where it rattled the ropes and curtain rods holding the soft, long, velvety red curtains that began to dance in the breeze.

A man walked onto the stage and looked around. The sunbeams made dust glisten and twirl in the air. He looked around the stage, up at the curtains and lights, then down at the chairs that would one day be filled with audiences waiting breathlessly for a play to begin.

"She is truly glorious," he said. "We must call her Gloria."

And so, my life as Gloria began.

People, known as the audience, tall and small, entered through the grand doors, walked down the aisles, and sat in the soft chairs row on row. The performers, whom I had become familiar with, were remarkable people. They entered into my auditorium like everyone else, but then transformed themselves into new people through their clothing, costumes, and fluctuating voices. I was almost overwhelmed at times, by what they could do.

Many times, a new collection of people sat close to my stage and played a wonderful assortment of small structures known as instruments. The sounds that were created often enticed the actors to match their voices with the instruments, or caused them to dance and sway around the stage. The heavenly music evoked every emotion possible in the performers and the audience time and time again. Oh, how I loved to see the variety of emotions on the faces of everyone during a performance.

Sometimes it was the hush of the actors, the quiet footsteps across the stage floor, the glimpse of an actor towards the audience from behind one of the red velvety curtains on a dimly lit stage, that evoked the biggest reactions from the audience.

For years, actors ran, walked, danced and crawled across my stage. They whispered, spoke eloquent poetry, sang hilarious songs, or screamed in horror as countless stories were told. The audiences let out shrieks of delight, gasps of awe, and exploded into raucous applause as each story unfolded before their eyes.

I loved every movement, every moment, every breath of being Gloria. Even when the actors seemed sad at times, or when more and more days passed between plays. The music, the smells and the sounds around me changed over the years, but I always cherished everyone and everything within me.

As the years passed by, the color on the walls and doors faded, except where sun and stage light did not touch them. The lights inside started to lose their shimmer. The floor made more noise when the occasional person walked across it. The filled auditorium of yesteryear had faded away.

One last play was performed. It was called Gloria. One final time when the performers' voices filled every space of my auditorium, my theatre. Each act was a glimpse of past performances, songs, and dances; a celebration of my life. I breathed in every moment of the final performance to hold within me forever.

One last curtain call. A final beautiful gathering of laughter, tears, gasps, and joy, shared with performers and audience alike.

This was my amazing life. I was the talk of the town. I was glorious. I still am. For the wind that plays its music on my stage, for the dance of the tattered curtains, and for all who hold memories of all that I have been. I am Gloria.

prompt: 1st person story of an old, abandoned theatre

A pencil poem

SHAWN L. BIRD

At first, a tree
Earth touching, sky reaching
So much to convey:
milled for messaging.
Ground down by circumstance,
miles of messages scribbled and scratched.
Sharp when it counts.
Seek the secrets of earth and sky:
Tree knowing.
We all make mistakes.
Erase.
Erase.
Draw roots on leaves.

Try again.
Leaden life?
New ideas.
New possibilities.
At the end well used
return to ground
nourish the earth.

prompt: a pencil

This Is How It Will All End

JANET L WHITEHEAD

G ATHERING OF THE UNIVERSAL Caretaker Council
Date: October 15 2024 - Earth time
Subject: Managing a multitude of crises on Earth
In attendance: Full council of 9 Universal Caretakers
Observed and documented by: The Official Teller
Note: *In accordance with Policy A55-2B – The Official
Teller is required to only observe and record. The Official Teller
acknowledges that they overstepped boundaries in this telling
and, also, requests to be appointed the Universal Storyteller in
the future as, clearly, this would be a much better fit.*

The gathering space is much like mortals might imagine the room for a meeting of Universal Caretakers. Centered in the room is a grand oak table circled by nine tall back chairs. A sooty stone fireplace fills a wall. The open windows reveal a view of various solar systems and endless stars.

The details would be harder for mortals to imagine. Flames in the fireplace flicker in dancing forms. There are images of wolves, faeries, trees, and a gathering of mortals in the flames. The mortal images are angry. Their flames are harsh and screaming. Carvings across the wood slats of the chairbacks move in time with the dancing flames. A mortal would call it a trick of lighting, except for the young mortals – they would see the stories evolve as carvings gently shift and change. The table itself is divided into nine pie shapes. There is paper and writing tools and brushes and pots of colour scattered in disarray. On a quieter day, these items would be neatly aligned for each chair and each pie shape. Today is not that day. Today is a day to change the course of humanity.

The Universal Caretakers materialize in each chair. They had stepped aside briefly so the Teller could document the setting for this event. Though the Teller seldom gets this kind of support, this is a day they have agreed must be immortalized. Whatever way it evolves, humankind will not be the same and there could well be some explaining to do.

The Caretakers – some are much like mortals might imagine them to be. God, Goddess-like, flowing robes, flowing hair, shimmering crowns of jewels and gold; but that's just two of them. There's also Bob who looks like the fellow who owns and operates the corner service station - back when someone operated a gas station and everyone got to know them. Bob has his 1950 style grey jacket, logo on a pocket; a bold embroidered *Bob's Garage* and in tiny print, *Gas and Gypsy Caravan Mechanic.* He's drumming his fingers on the table, his pen set down beside a large paper full of chicken-scratched calculations.

The two God and Goddess-like beings are more busy basking in a breeze flowing through their hair than paying attention to anything on the table. They will not be pleased with that statement when they discover it. The Teller must, however, tell what the Teller witnesses. The Teller mustn't include their own opinions, like that the god, goddess-like beings really are a token addition to the group. Visually acceptable to the mortals, but really, so full of themselves that they aren't helpful. But the Teller mustn't mention those things.

Morgan, the Master of the Earthly Realm, is the historian of Earth and its inhabitants. Morgan is dressed in the latest Earth fashion of high waist jeans, a crop top t-shirt, and a streak of blue in otherwise white hair.

Morgan speaks, "Remember, they, too, are masters. Anyone choosing to play the mortal game on Earth are masters from other realms and times. Humanity is the greatest game and greatest challenge of all, given that they choose to arrive on Earth with no memory. They deserve our respect."

"Ah, dear Master of the Looneyverse," Celeste, the Celestial Traffic Controller, says. All those seated at the table snicker, including Morgan. Even the Teller snickers at this fitting title for Earth.

"And do we just watch them keep playing the game?" Celeste, in her gown of swirling stars, continues, "Or shall I toss Earth off kilter, hurl her out of her galaxy, ensure an early explosion... call her done and let something new grow from the remnants?"

At this, they all guffaw. "The celestial sky is crashing and supernova-ing all the time, not because you plan it that way," Bob says, "but because you are off sipping lattes or highland dancing and ignoring your job!"

"Perhaps," Celeste replies, "And perhaps we put too much work into controlling things. Perhaps we should all sip a good strong brandy latte, pop up some popcorn and just watch what those crazy mortals do next."

The entire room hushes when Paul, the Pinwheel Universe Engineer, stands up. He is in his usual attire, a well-worn lab coat. Known as the creator of the unexpected, he will spin the wildest ideas together, while mumbling, 'What if...' He was the instigator of the whole Earth project. The entire room is hushed hoping Paul takes some responsibility for the craziness.

"The unexpected is what makes Earth and all her living things so clever, adapting as things change. But now, it's unacceptable to expect the place to adapt to this degree of unexpected," Paul looks down in shame. "About a century ago I did do a wee little extra bit of unexpectedness... you know, just for fun. I'm sorry. It seems to have spun quite wildly out of control."

"Ah ha!" Morgan exclaims, "In the past, major changes and events happened unexpectedly every century or so. Earth had time to adjust. But then things started happening every decade, then every year, then every month, week, and now... well, there's a crisis every minute, it seems."

"Oh hell," mumbles Celeste, "I thought things were a bit boring back then, too. I gave Earth a little off kilter twist for kicks."

Bob gave them all a withering glance and returned to his calculations.

"Okay, we better fess up, too," God and Goddess spoke in unison, "We haven't had the respect we deserve since Mesopotamia! We may have gotten a little annoyed with the devotion to money above all else and dropped a curse or two or, um, maybe more, during this century."

Bob stood up; his hands firmly planted on the table. "Well done, you dingbats! The numbers exponentially say there is no hope they can pull through this mess and the suffering will be immense!"

The Teller cannot record the next moments accurately with the cacophony that erupts in the room as a result of these confessions. There are other Caretakers in each of the nine chairs who are not yet reported in this telling. They are, however, engaged in the loud expressions of concern and questions bouncing off the walls. There is much thinking going on that involves the tossing of pencils and paintbrushes. The Caretakers live in the realm of compassion, curiosity, appreciation for each other's uniqueness, and excellent communication abilities. It is their nature. Today, though, the voices and flying pencils have rather loud hints of outrage and judgement. The teller notes the behaviour is rather human. It is a very unusual day.

The only quiet is the fireplace, as if it has paused to listen. The images on the backs of the chairs have also paused, as if the story has stopped, anticipating the next paragraph. The Teller notes this has never happened in the history of forever so far.

Even while the arguments and accusations continue, the Caretakers have been glancing furtively at Eleh, the D.S.D. The Teller speculates that she will be the one to come up with the final answer in this complex situation. Although it will be frowned upon that the Teller is reporting an opinion, the Teller feels an explanation is due as to why all the participants keep glancing expectantly at the D.S.D. They, too, are counting on her. Her initials, D.S.D, stand for detective, scientist, and doodler. Eleh is furiously doodling on a large square of parchment. As is her nature, the more the group shares ideas, the more information gathered, the more she doodles. The more she doodles, the more likely her creative investigative and scientific mind will reveal an answer. It's how the D.S.D works. A doodling lateral thinker.

Morgan flinches when Eleh draws emphatic scribbles across everything she has doodled on the paper so far, scribbles so harsh that the paper begins to tear. "This is not good," Morgan whispers.

The others stop their talking and pencil tossing when the D.S.D starts stabbing her paper.

"This is how it will end," Eleh, the D.S.D, mumbles.

All is still in the room. Waiting. Watching as the D.S.D now slowly draws spirals on the page. The Celestial Traffic Controller hesitantly whispers, "Ends? I wasn't serious about..." but her voice chokes mid-sentence. A rare tear forms in her eye.

The flames stretch beyond the fireplace to watch the drawing. Images on the chairbacks extend over the top and turn to witness how it will all end.

Eleh begins to draw swirling lines that form the shape of hearts. She fills each corner of the parchment with this shape. She adds more, then adds exclamation marks beside each one. The Teller has a feeling of hope. The Teller is not supposed to have feelings which is why the Teller can report occurrences so accurately. Today, though, in this moment, the Teller feels hope.

Eleh drops her pencil and looks up. She gazes from one Caretaker to the next, ensuring she has the entire room's attention. She takes a moment to observe the images in the fire and on each chairback. She gives them a nod and a gentle smile.

"This is how it will all end," Eleh, the D.S.D, announces, "This is how we will end the chaos. We will give them back their memories."

The impact of this concept filters its way through the room. The room is still silent, but the Teller notes eyes brightening, frowns dissipating, strained shoulders visibly relaxing and a few jaws dropping open. Flames and chairback images appear confused as they observe the room.

The Teller blurts out, "They will remember. They will know the magnificent immortal beings that they are!" The Teller turns to the flames and the chairback images, "Yours will be a beautiful story now. Glorious, even!" The Teller is sorry to say that the Teller leaps about the room dancing;

this is entirely inappropriate behaviour. The Teller pauses, shocked at their own breach of the responsibilities of the Teller.

The Caretakers burst out in laughter and cheers.

"What the heck, let's all dance!" Bob calls out, and with a snap of his fingers, *Jailhouse Rock* entices everyone into a rock and rolling dancing celebration.

And thus, the dancing Universal Caretakers celebrate the end of life on Earth as it is currently known and the beginning of something so much greater.

The Caretakers then set to work, many souls working as one, to make the previously unthinkable, delightfully do-able. The Teller notes: It is a good end.

———ele———

Prompts:
Alternate Identity Trading Cards
Paint Chip Poetry prompt: 'This is how it will all end.'

About the Authors

Holly Alford

Holly is as lost as Alice and as mad as the Hatter. She is occupied by doing as she pleases and dabbles in all sorts of artistic pursuits including writing, encaustic art, and jewelry making but she specializes in confidential creativity. Holly would love to tell you more about it, but that's confidential. Holly has also been known to chronicle some of her life and adventures on her blog eccentricelena.com

Shawn L. Bird

Shawn is a high school English teacher, author, and poet in the beautiful Shuswap region of British Columbia.

She is the author of several novellas, novels, short stories and poetry collections. Her novella length interconnected noir short story collection *Murdering Mr. Edwards* was nominated for an Arthur Ellis Crime Writers Award. Her YA fantasy series *Grace Awakening* was nominated for a Whistler Independent Book Award. You're invited to visit her at ShawnBird.com.

Valerie Dawn

Valerie is a 74 year old grandmother who began writing 5 years ago. An Australian Canadian, she has lived with her husband in Kamloops since 1976. She writes poetry inspired by nature and relationships, and received an honourable mention in the Very Short Verse Poetry Competition, Canadian League of Poets, 2019. Valerie Dawn is writing two memoirs, plus reflections on covid times, spirituality, nature, and healing. She can be reached at valeriedawn70@gmail.com

Jessica Hewlett

Jessica is a juggler of too many hobbies who procrastinates with gaming when she really ought to be focusing on the plethora of ideas that her brain spews out. Her favourite writing exercises are word prompts. Give her a genre, character, and subject and her mind explodes with stories. Jessica's current projects: a ten-year-old novel she's wrangling into completion about Oxford, a living shadow, and the woman caught in-between; a new novel about the consequences of a bee sting; and her latest night of the living dead rodeo clown short story.

Kristy Janota

Kristy is a Kamloops real estate agent and accountant who dabbles in writing in her spare time. She has a passion for supporting people to improve their lives and has published a children's book called "Find Your Happy." Currently in process, she is writing a non-fiction book for the adults with tips to thrive and stay calm in this busy world. She enjoys spending time with her husband, kids, and their funny little dog. Kristy is constantly learning, making essential oil concoctions, reading, and watching fiction - especially fiction with a mystical twist.

Mary Jordan

Mary is a long-time journal writer and story catcher. Her joy in writing is weaving memories of her travels and family history into stories. Her current passion is spinning family folklore into a historic legacy. Besides creating memories in her own time, she also likes to ask

the ancestors to speak. Find her at RareBirds Housing
Co-operative and on Facebook.

Shannon Lalonde

Shannon was born, raised, and currently lives in Calgary,
Alberta. She'll soon be celebrating 25 years of marriage and
she is mother to 2 fabulous children. Shannon has been
inspiring elementary school children for almost 30 years.
She loves theatre, music, dancing, and story writing.

Coreena McBurnie

A scholar of the ancient mysteries, Coreena lives in
the land of northern lights and maple syrup with her
clan and feline overlords. Fueled by herbal infusions and
chocolate as dark as her heart, she spends time shrouded
in self doubt, reading the pages of scribes, befriending
dragons, and chasing rainbows and shiny things like a
deranged magpie, while scribbling random musings that
sometimes amount to something. A book of her words
haunts dark corners of libraries and the internet. You may
find her sporadically on Instagram @CoreenaMcBurnie or
FaceBook @CoreenaMcBurnie,author.

Janet L. Whitehead

Janet is writer, artist, and a lifelong advocate for the creative soul. She is the owner and curator of Writerly Kits and is a professional creativity coach, leading retreats and workshops for 15 years. She is also rather passionate about her grandchildren, the great outdoors, and tall ships. Oh, and magic – her memoir, *Beyond All Imaginings*, tells that story. Learn more: novelminds.ca or musingsandmud.com.